A PARRAGON BOOK
Published by Parragon Book Service Ltd, Unit 13-17 Avonbridge Trading Estate,
Atlantic Road, Avonmouth, Bristol BS11 9QD
Produced by The Templar Company plc, Pippbrook Mill,
London Road, Dorking, Surrey RH4 1JE
ISBN 0-75250-887-3

Goldilocks

Illustrated by Brian Bartle

‖ •PARRAGON• ‖

Once upon a time there were three who lived in a little in the middle of the . There was a mummy , a daddy and a baby .

Every morning they had of porridge for breakfast, but one day their was too hot to eat. So the three went for a walk in the while it cooled down.

While they were gone a little called Goldilocks passed by. She knocked at the and found no one home, so she went inside. There she found three of porridge on the .

First 🧒 tried the big 🥣 of porridge, but it was too salty. Then she tried the medium 🥣, but it was too sweet. Finally she tried the little 🥣 of porridge. It was just right!

Naughty ate it all up, then went to sit down. She tried the big , but it was too hard. Then she tried the medium , but it was too soft. Then she tried the baby .

It was just right! But the
sweet little broke into
pieces, so naughty went
upstairs to find a .

The big was too high,
the medium was too low.

But the little was just right! curled up and soon fell asleep.

The came home and saw someone had been there.

"Someone's been eating my

porridge!" said .

"Someone's been eating my

porridge!" said .

"Someone's been eating my

porridge," squeaked ,

"and they've eaten it all up!"

Then they saw the chairs.

Mummy and daddy's

had only been sat in, but the

little was broken to pieces!

"Someone's been sitting in

my ," said .

"Someone's been sitting in my 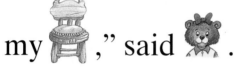 ," said 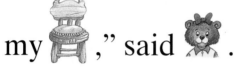 .

"Someone's been sitting in my and it's broken !" cried .

They crept upstairs.

"Someone's been sleeping in

my ," said .

"Someone's been sleeping in my ," said .

"Someone's been sleeping in my ," said , "and they're still there!"

At the sound of nigh

squeaky voice, woke up in

a fright.

She fled from the ,

and was never seen in those

 again!